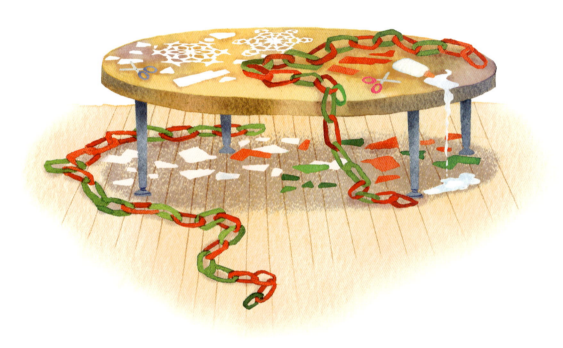

To Dave, who understands the
power of wishes and of believing
—M.L.

For Emma, thank you for sharing
your adventures
—T.M.

Ho Ho Homework
Text copyright © 2019 by Mylisa Larsen
Illustrations copyright © 2019 by Taia Morley
All rights reserved. Manufactured in China.
No part of this book may be used or reproduced in any manner whatsoever without written permission
except in the case of brief quotations embodied in critical articles and reviews. For information address
HarperCollins Children's Books, a division of HarperCollins Publishers, 195 Broadway, New York, NY 10007.
www.harpercollinschildrens.com

ISBN: 978-0-06-279688-2
Library of Congress Control Number: 2018959776

The artist used watercolor and traditional media with Adobe
Photoshop to create the digital illustrations for this book.
Typography by Erica De Chavez
19 20 21 22 23 SCP 10 9 8 7 6 5 4 3 2 1 ❖ First Edition

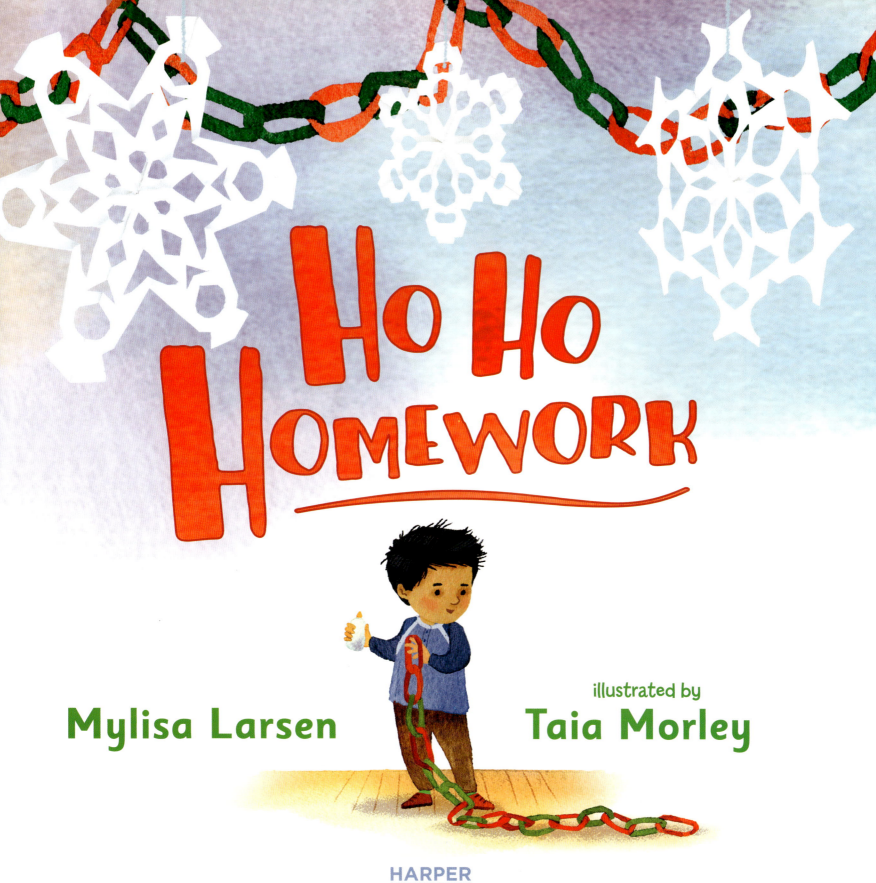

Ho Ho Homework

Mylisa Larsen

illustrated by

Taia Morley

HARPER

An Imprint of HarperCollinsPublishers

For weeks, Jack looked out every window he passed.

Waiting for snow.

Wishing.

But there was not one flurry. Not even a flake.

On this morning, Jack felt hopeful.
"There's lots of clouds today," said his
friend Rosa. "I bet it will snow today."
"Maybe," said Jack.

When they got to school, no one was paying attention to the weather. All anyone could talk about was the new substitute teacher.

Hello, my name Mr. Clausen

"Look at his beard," said Rosa.
"And his boots," said Leo.

But Jack wasn't so sure.
"Just because he has a white
beard, doesn't mean it's him."

1. cut strips

2. put a DOT of glue on one end.

3. Glue ends together.

Jack did notice that Mr. Clausen
was more patient than most teachers.

When Houdini got out, Mr. Clausen's
big laugh left most of the kids wide-eyed.

" I don't know, Jack," said Leo.
"It sounded a lot like a 'ho, ho, ho'
to me."

But Jack still wasn't so sure.

At lunch, Jack and Leo peeked in through the window of the teacher's lounge. "Cookies and milk," reported Leo.

"So what?" said Jack. "Everybody likes cookies. That doesn't mean anything."

"Jack," said Leo. "The cookies were shaped like reindeer."

During quiet time, the kids kept a close watch on Mr. Clausen. "Why is he making socks?" Jack whispered to Rosa.

THE NORTH POLE

"Stockings, Jack," Rosa said. "Those are stockings."

And Mr. Clausen did seem to be making a whole lot of lists.

During science, Jack got looks from all over the room. "So he likes sleds," said Jack. "Everybody likes sleds."

"Not teachers," said Leo. "Not *that* much."

HOW TO MAKE A PAPER SNOWFLAKE

1. FOLD
2. FOL
3. FOL
4. FOL

5. CUT AROUND EDGES of

That afternoon, Mr. Clausen taught everyone how to make paper snowflakes.

"Make a snowflake and write a wish on the back," he said. "That's your homework."

The next day, Mr. Clausen talked to the class about wishes. Everyone hung their snowflakes all over the room. Everyone except Jack.

But as Jack looked around the classroom, even he had to admit that things were pretty cheerful. Some kids were decorating Houdini's cage. Tim and Evan were getting along and that *never* happened.

And Mr. Clausen was doing the jingle bell
shuffle. It was nice. It was almost . . . merry.

At the end of the day, Mr. Clausen walked out with the kids to say goodbye. "Wow," said Rosa. "That is a really big backpack." It was.

"Just a minute," said Jack.
"This is for you."

"Why, thank you, Jack," said Mr. Clausen. And for just an instant, Jack thought Mr. Clausen's eyes twinkled.

That evening, Jack taught his sisters how to cut out snowflakes. He was really patient.

On Christmas Eve, he helped them put out milk and cookies.

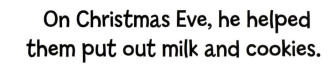

Then he showed them how to do the jingle bell shuffle.

And as he lay in bed that night, Jack thought and thought about his wish.

On Christmas morning, Jack opened
one eye and looked out his window.
Then he opened both eyes wide.

"Come and see! Come and see!" he shouted.

And that day, the whole neighborhood enjoyed Jack's wish.
Especially Jack.

my wish is snow

You can make a paper snowflake like the one Jack made. Be sure to get a grown-up to help you with the scissors. Follow the instructions below to make a snowflake. When you are done, think of a wish and write it in the middle of your snowflake.

Tape a piece of string to your snowflake and hang it on your tree or by your bed. Your snowflake wish can be a new family tradition!

HOW TO MAKE A
PAPER SNOWFLAKE

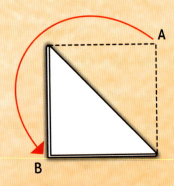

1. Begin with a square piece of paper. Fold the paper diagonally, bringing the corner A to corner B.

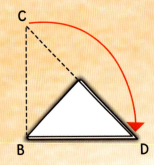

2. Fold corner C to corner D.

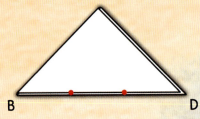

3. Make two marks on the long side of your folded triangle so the long side is marked into equal thirds.

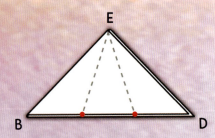

4. Draw two light lines from the top point (E) of the triangle to the marks on the long side of your triangle.

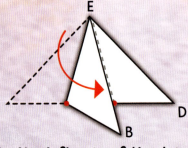

5. Fold the left side of the triangle over along the right line.

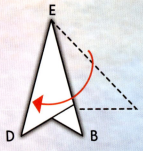

6. Fold the right side over along the other line.

7. Cut off the bottom.

8. Make cuts on all three sides of the triangle. But don't cut the tip of the triangle so you'll have room to write your wish!

9. Carefully unfold your snowflake and now write your wish!